I0581985

Self Portrait
as Vanishing Act

Leslie Ullman

LILY POETRY REVIEW BOOKS

Praise for Leslie Ullman

Natural Histories, Yale University Press, 1979

"In her honest, quiet way, Ullman puts to poetic use the self-generating power that lies within her. No restraint is so permanent it cannot be cast off, no confinement so total release cannot be won. Her freedom is the ideal freedom of the poet, the mind going on, distilling, adding, converting, supplementing and complementing, certain of the real relationship of response to event no matter how remote or peripheral the events are or how ineffectual or unrelated the responses seem. Reading Natural Histories, many times, I've come to feel her freedom is my freedom."

—Richard Hugo

Dreams by No One's Daughter, University of Pittsburgh Press, 1987

"In her new volume, Dreams by No One's Daughter, Leslie Ullman traces with characteristic grace the urgencies of one's passage through a life—from the fabular weathers of childhood into those hard climes of adulthood, and along the endless currents of dream. There is a quiet, a composure here that is both beautiful and disarming. Contemplative, precise, these poem instruct us in the delights of their world."

—David St. John

Slow Work Through Sand, University of Iowa Press (winner of the Iowa Poetry Prize), 1998

"In a delightful poem titled 'French,' Leslie Ullman speaks of 'the mother river of language flowing past….' She uses it to bring contrasting landscapes to life: northern island, southern desert, both infused with the colors and textures of uncut gems."

—Maxine Kumin

"Leslie Ullman has the ability to spin illuminating spells through and around the matter of earth and life. Her vision penetrates with an attention as careful and as transforming as day through clear water, as moonlight on stone. She is an artisan with words, and the results are poems embodying the intricacy and beauty of the subjects they honor."

—Pattiann Rogers

Progress on the Subject of Immensity, University of New Mexico Press, 2013

"For thirty years now, Leslie Ullman has steadily refined a poetry of the most acute and lyrically precise mindfulness, of what one of her poems calls the 'greater alertness.' This method has been forged in part by her ability to render the harsh beauties of the southwestern landscapes that have been her adopted home. More important still, however, is her almost shamanistic willingness to visit those liminal states between waking and dreaming, conventional reality and phantasm—states that sometimes offer menace, sometimes wonderment. This is all to say that Leslie Ullman is a poet of the first order, writing at the height of her very considerable powers."

—David Wojahn

Little Soul and The Selves, 3:TaosPress, October, 2023

"In her poetic sequence, *Little Soul and the Selves*, Leslie Ullman offers a rich and rewarding commentary on the multiplicity of roles life demands of us and the undefinable, but felt unity of consciousness that underlies them. To browse the list of poem titles alone is delicious: "Little Soul Remembers," "Little Soul Comes Across Lines by George Seferis," "The Selves Channel the Day the Parents Met," "If Little Soul and the Selves Were a Rock Band . . ." Playfully side-stepping the perils of direct philosophical inquiry, Ullman avoids the weighty "I" of confession and turns autobiography into a series of adventures, a profound questioning of human identity and the forces that tear at it. These are supple, athletic poems, full of the thisness of the world, touching lightly and with elegance on the larger questions."

—Jean Nordhaus

"Who knew 21st-century soul-searching could cast such a spell? In this beguiling sequence, poet Leslie Ullman searches through the relics of her past, reassembling a private world with patience and precision. As readers, we enter it as if it were our own. Bringing ancestry, demography, philosophy, and Jungian psychology into play, Ullman summons vanished time, 'seeing it afresh.' Open to any page, and "the ghosts come forward / through image, through dream, through / meandering guess." With its comic turns and keen-eyed observations, *Little Soul and the Selves* considers the meaning of a singular life and not only asks *Who am I?* but also poses the hardest question: *What is the nature of a human soul?*"

—Jody Bolz

Unruly Tree, University of New Mexico Press, 2024

"Because there is no shrugging of 'the weight and shame/or being *human*,' the gift that Leslie Ullman's *Unruly Tree* offers is precious, as over and over its poems 'glimpse/something diamond pure/for a moment in ourselves.'"

—Harvey L. Hix

Table of Contents

Self Portrait as a Jigsaw Puzzle

From a distance I seem
                 to be holding
                       myself
        together
as meadow
      patchworked with
          bluebells   poppies   goldenrod
or seascape rent by rain-filled
                 clouds
                   white-capped waves
           vessel in full sail
                    struggling to
   right itself
or splashes   swirls
       of Monet   Van Gogh   ever
             faithful to
                  masterpiece
        barely hanging on to
                 myself
         don't
           jostle me   wait
                  to find
       fit that will never be
                fusion
no matter what
     you "see"
         I am always
     in pieces.

Self Portrait as Display of Relics

I have held water, encircled a woman's
wrist, ground grains against stone
or turned land for seeding.
I am tarnished gold.
Chipped clay. Iron shaped
by flame and blunt force.

Sometimes I was pewter tankard
holding mead at tables laden with
trenchers, sometimes jeweled chalice
for Communion wine—the one exquisite
object in a village whose inhabitants wore
homespun, and covered their windows

with sacking that let in draughts.
I have lived in the coffers of monasteries
raided again and again, passing into
the hands of invaders and sometimes
returning. I have stood in for saints,
the Word of God, and God Himself.

In my presence, the needy received cures
because they believed they would. Now, I
dwell where centuries of ice once groaned across
the land and left layers of soil. Sometimes
a shard of me has surfaced, gleaming
under a trowel and lifted gently to be

dated, catalogued, and placed under glass
and strong light. No one knows how much of me
remains in darkness, where I prefer the company
of other secrets, and where my origins in the hands
of ancient artisans dissolve into my true origins:
rock worked by upheaval, water and wind.

Self Portrait as a Joker

The deck I belong to misses essential cards: perhaps
I replace one, or none, perhaps I trick you

into changing the rules or throwing down
your hand in pique or boredom or as prelude

to something else, a cocktail or cold swim…. I am not
to be trusted. I take no offense, knowing my presence

derails what you were dealt, and all bets
are off unless I can fill in for an Ace of Spades

or Jack of Diamonds when you need
a power move, straight flush, or amped-up bluff.

I slap you with my grin, my brimmed hat cocked
in devil-may-care, when I turn up in your hand—

especially if you're another bridge-addicted
matron who thought she had put me face-down

in a drawer smelling of pennies and old pencils—but
now what?—play cool, or replace the deck?

I call my own shots. I shapeshift as I please. I'll not disappear
in the face of bad press, dancing to a drum you can't hear.

Self Portrait as a Weather Map

I should be reliable, backed as I am by satellites,
antennae probing the air as though attached
to perceptive crustaceans, and trained meteorologists
who accessorize their reports with cheerful voices,
skilled tailoring, and sculpted hair which likely
is dyed or streaked—I have no quarrel there—
if I had hair, I'd do it too

but I do enjoy proving them wrong—
straightening the curve of jet stream
a degree or two, moving cloud cover a tad east
or west, or skewing slightly the wind's actual
mph just enough to keep everyone guessing
when a storm will make landfall or a blizzard
shut down the routes to gas and canned goods.

In truth, I revere the mystery of atmospherics,
their blend of cosmic muscle and choreographies
shaped by sea coasts and mountain chains,
phenomena humans haven't yet
tamed, which may be why they like to watch
channels devoted to what's blowing or falling
even across regions they aren't living in.

I beguile them with statistics, wind-arrows and cloud-
blobs colored according to moisture content
and temperature. They think I know when precipitation
will leave their little patch of globe in time for a picnic
or daily run. It settles them to check me multiple
times a day, and I pretend to help, while relishing
what indifferent, magnificent ferocities prevail.

Self Portrait as a Vermeer Painting

I am window, third eye into the family dwelling
that directs, by illumination, your gaze
towards the peripheral—not the face of the woman

bent to her piano keys, but the mirror's reflection
of her tilted cheek; not the dim passage to a squalid
kitchen yard, but the milkmaid's alabaster brow

bent to her pitcher releasing milk-gleam
of white touched with blue. The dew-shine
of young skin. The flare-dot on a sable eye

as daylight angles across it…. I am caressed
by the gaze and brush of a man who
fathered eleven and might have wished

to escape his fecund household for a tankard
and raucous talk, but sought instead my quiet
interiors and their inhabitants whose faces

are soft with solitude and singular thought
as they lower their eyes to a letter or book, and you
are the voyeur invited into these privacies.

I am the still point where angles meet
like star glints to direct your gaze towards
my center, though you are

unaware of this. Jerrybuilt
of patience and careful layers
of illusion, I am unequivocally real.

Self Portrait as a Lab Experiment

I began as purple water and minor explosions
created by a budding chemist given her first set—
accidents, all—then was nuanced, enlarged, among
titrates, tubes, Petrie dishes, and beakers in rooms
smelling of ammonia and burnt matches.

I've been parsed again and again along grids
of the Periodic Table, then reassembled under
strong lights on squares of glass, by acolytes
hoping to stumble on cures for cancer, birth defects
and old age. On occasion, someone's politics

have shut me down. Animal rights nudged me
away from living mice, monkeys, and dogs—
this eased me—I prefer the nerveless dance
of molecules, the fissions and fusions
between them, and stem cells called in

like calvary to change the course of illness
and reverse wear and tear. I thrive on inquiry
and speculation. I believe in limitless possibility.
I have waited years for numbers to coalesce
to statistics that can't be ignored—

given time, I could make you live forever.

Self-Portrait as Metropolis

I am all angle and asphalt, impenetrable
as Achilles' shield, cross-streets quarrelsome
and clotted with traffic trying, trying to get
somewhere, like bee-swarms caught in their own

maelstroms—too many hives here, which way
is home? Sunlight glints off black windows,
pinched seeds set in rows against the skyline.
I ignite ambitions fulfilled and then forgotten,

chronic longing and impatience so ingrained
even a stoplight causes cortisol spike and flare
of ulcer. I am lines at the deli, the corner of Madison
and 47th, the post office, the bus, and congestion

on sidewalks where the locals have mastered duck-and-
dodge, holding their satchels close. They all wear black
or beige, but for a smattering of children in pastels or neon….
Some days, when weather makes its way through

as snowfall or serious rain, I am briefly softened
or polished, moisture tamping the exhalations
of subway grates and muting the noise of drills
battling concrete. My elevators, vertical trunks rising

from a network of basements, smell of wet wool.
But there's a giddiness, some message from another world
to shake off umbrellas or stamp off boots—expectation
that can't be grasped—daydream of soft soil and new

or dormant green, a crack in my shield, a transport.
Soon, when summer thunder rolls over the spikes
and shafts that bristle me, I too may relinquish a bit
of what I have tensed and hardened into.

Self Portrait as the Poem I Could Never Write

I might be edgy, experimental, and of mixed
lineage.

My preferred pronoun might be up for grabs.

I might speak from a culture whose written
language comes across to English speakers

as beautiful hieroglyphics; perhaps was born

in a place where women cover their faces
or know how to balance jars on their heads;

perhaps journeyed across a desert

or in the hold of a boat; might be the first in the family
to speak English; suffered

bullies, bigots, assaults, and ignorant teachers

and then went to Harvard. All this
would be grist for writings now revered

by a culture trying mightily to grow up,

a culture well-intentioned and eager
as a Labrador puppy rolling over

and over on its back before the troubled peoples

of its not-world—the ravaged districts, the starvelings,
the queers, the silenced—

as though it were harmless.

In the poem I'll never be, the words are every shade
but white, the music jarring and hard to forget.

It prods and mocks and does not suffer fools

even as it has learned to live among them.
They want the cudgel, they want

the taking-down. They think they will grow up

and be forgiven if they take it in. It knows better
but keeps cracking the whip.

Self Portrait as a Family Heirloom

I am Artemis or Diana, a young doe lying
at my feet, my palm poised above her nose
in mid-caress, and she meets my eyes
because she trusts me. Both of us
are lithe and fine-boned, our bond
preserved in white porcelain.
My breasts are small, my waist attenuated
and slender—I could well be a boy,
so easy am I in near-nakedness, my skin
smooth over long muscle—I could well be
a deer. So how is it I ended up

among books, tweeds, and silver ash trays
in an uptown apartment smelling of lemon oil
and pipe smoke, placed beneath a porcelain lamp
the color of dark berries? And what appealed
to the tightly coiffed wife and Very Important
husband with his trimmed mustache
and silver-tipped cane who came upon me
in a Paris shop full of lace and crystal?
My short locks have never seen a comb, feathering
away from my brow even as I tilt my head downward
to hold the gaze of my wild friend, my eyes soft,
my mouth in a near-smile gentle as my touch.

They knew beauty. But the little girl
who came and left over the years, who spent
long moments gazing at me as though
reading a book, shared my prized solitude.
She received me receiving the deer, the deer
receiving me, and carried our image into her future
as a talisman against The Taming of Girls.
In time, I came to her wrapped in foam
and nested in a box, one slender ear of my doe

broken off, soon glued securely but leaving
a scar. Like what the years have done
to that granddaughter's skin as she heads into
all weathers, receiving each season's silence, waiting
for any shy creature willing to come close, asking
no solution to the mystery that will never
entirely breach the space between them.

Self Portrait as a Thrift Store Find

If there were more than one of me
I would have been found in Consignment,
real crystal that I am, Baccarat or Orrefors
or Waterford, my label long gone,
my provenance unknown.

I once was a family of twelve designed
to hold white wine to go with soup or fish
before being whisked away for the big players,
Beef Wellington or Bourgogne, and a hearty
Bordeaux flown in from France.

No one serves five courses anymore
or wants crystal or has servants, and no
matter the art of making me goes back
2,000 years and has little changed. Silica-
sand, potash, and red-lead—you'd never guess

these coalesce into my exquisite
see-through-ness, or that when oxygen
is driven off from red-lead oxide you get
a yellow oxide called "lethargy," another part
of the mystery I am made of.

I've found a new home among vessels chosen
one by one from displays of dusty ball jars
and juice glasses printed with daisies or decals
of Mickey Mouse and Pluto. I dwell unmatched
in a cabinet with three cobalt goblets and a chipped

green vase. I most often am placed beside a shade-
covered lawn chair, or on a scuffed wooden table
beside a book. Given my mineral origins, I am
oddly warm to the touch. If you run a finger
along my rim, I still sing.

Self Portrait as an Epitaph

I share a profound stillness with those departed—
my silence in stone, theirs underground.
I am birth-and-death dates—and sometimes the word
beloved—beneath formal names rarely used,
the lifelong nicknames now interred with those
who bore them in pleasure or chagrin.

Everything I have to say has been
worked into stone and now exists as fraught
silence rising like breath in the minds of those
who roam past my plinth in drizzle or dappled
shade, subdued, among so many finished lives
and the mystery of their rest.

I reveal nothing of meals savored or hastily
consumed, celebrations, disappointments, flesh
warming flesh in shared beds, betrayals, bearings-
up, inner lives grown vast and undetected over
decades, now forever unknown. I leave speculation
to those who may pause before me where I lean

over tended grass and a metropolis of endings.
Ever faithful to fact, I am the keeper of secrets
that can neither be proved nor disputed—that flare
and subside but never disappear. Reading me, some
might imagine what I know and do not say:
absolute, the veil between worlds.

Self Portrait as Bowling Pin-Setter

First there was a man a man in shirtsleeves
sweating, balding, retired from a job
as office clerk or mail-sorter, now
keeping busy in a venue for cheap beer
and friendly competition. He didn't expect
the endless din behind the lanes, the stress
of gathering swiftly, watching for wobble,
the violently-toppled pins, then placing them upright
again and again for impatient competitors.

Sometimes it was a young father baffled
by night feedings and worried about clogged
gutters, eager for the focus required by timing
so many physical tasks almost at once—
the choreography of gathering, re-setting pins
in formation, and sending heavy balls back to players
again and again, perfecting himself
as a fine-tuned machine.

Then I came along, *all* machine, a complex of
pulleys, sensors, conveyer belts, ejector flaps,
release levers, shark fin guides and setting
assembly, a feat of engineering so deft,
the genius of my workings bemuses anyone
who cares to look me up on YouTube.
I made my inventor a fortune. Ditto my distributor
whose bequests went to descendants who in turn
have patronized symphonies and museums

and one of whom keeps in her home (and has
promised to The Art Institute) a Miro, a Kandinsky,
a Picasso and a box by Joseph Cornell that holds

a yellow ball, half a white pipe, and a wineglass
containing a single blue marble. Her walls pulse
with line and color—marvelous, inexplicable—
more tributes to what humans can do
when they're not turning plowshares into swords.

Self Portrait as Penthesilia

Thracian queen, leader of the Amazon
battalion of women famously feared, I came
to the aid of Troy and for a time thwarted
the Achaeans holding their relentless siege.
I faced Achilles one on one, his equal
(and there were few) in wielding spear, sword
and shield, and I even killed him until Zeus
intervened. I had no male god to back me
but held my own to tip, for a moment, the balance
of that long war, while Helen and other wives,
maidens, and mothers waited, trembling
behind the barricades.

So he killed me, my death just another
disemboweling amid the slaughter
that became white noise in Homer's
revered epic—how could he have thought
such details mattered, blood spilled
and spilled, tears shed and shed for the fallen—
if anything, his opus makes a fine case
for the waste of war and the blindness
men mistake for courage....

You may wonder why I chose to take up weapons
and train an army of women. It was not
a taste for blood or power—
it was the full habitation of the body
and heart I was given—the stalwart legs
that carried me, sword in one hand
and shield in the other; the feint
and jab; the trained eye and aim; the thrill
of movement and rush of something like
fresh water moving through me even
when I was spent. Had I been born

in another time, I would have scaled
tall cliffs like a spider, or been leader
of five working together to drive a ball
through mesh enclosures in a dance
between sisters, dialogue beyond words—
or I'd have been a dancer known for grace so
fluid, so at one with muscle and limb, she gently
pierced others' hearts with a celebration
of what the body can do, and made them
glad to be dwelling in theirs.

Self Portrait as an Eraser

I spent first grade as a self-made smudge, eyes
averted below a cloud of brown frizz in the ancient

class photo. I was born with my head in the clouds.
Even I didn't know where to find it

and drifted elsewhere while the others made block
letters with thick pencils, taking their first steps

towards Merit Scholarships and the Ivy League.
First grade was my introduction to the line between

the gifted and the ordinary. The blonde pony-tailed
and the awkward. The leaders and the introverts.

One day, while laboring to get my a's and e's
to look like Susie N's who sat beside me

I found myself holding a crumpled oblong
of rubber I'd pressed too hard to clear the lined page

and start again. And again. The teacher, patient
Miss Vaughn, sent me to the supply room to ask for

a replacement, an *art gum eraser*, strange words I was afraid
I would lose during my solo walk down two hallways

to a room that smelled of new paper and chalk.
I sang it to myself, repeating *art gum*

eraser, art gum eraser, determined to quell
the anxiety—a word I didn't yet know—that settled

over me like a fog every time I did something new.
Art gum eraser, art gum eraser, crumbled rubber

and graphite blur, I was *art gum eraser.*

Self Portrait as *Fog Woman*

Those who knew me best in college called me that—
me, drifting from the dorm some nights to gaze

into strangers' lit kitchens, or traipsing
through town after a blizzard to photograph

what the sky had spilled over gate posts
and bird feeders, turning them to gnomes….

Perhaps my penchant for daydream
and random observations struck others

as spacy. Perhaps I lived more mindfully
in the word-spells of books than what the world

presented. I was bad at facial recognition
and remembering names, but otherwise

managed all right the world of weekend
mixers, dorm gossip over Mateus rosé

and academic tasks if they were open-ended
rather than True/False or Multiple-choice.

I still don't know what flew past me, what others
saw—me tuning out now and then? Nose in a novel?

Finding a human face or bison hump in cloud-mass
gathering overhead? Might such wanderings be taken

for clearing the air, making way for imagination
and random perception as… *pleasure?*

I was no genius. Not an obvious eccentric.
I should have asked my friends what they saw.

From my fog—it that's what it was—I can say I remain
in thrall to the big sky the mind is.

Self Portrait as an O'Keeffe Flower

I was never what the critics proclaimed—
they never touched the core of me, those smug
assumptions that swirled and swelled until they
self-combusted over tepid wine and canapés
at gallery openings, and filled the columns of *Art Forum*
and *Art News* with Freudian jargon, condescension
and self-importance. I stayed out of it—as did
O'Keeffe. She removed herself to a high-desert
dwelling made of straw and mud, where the light
worked its magic over uninhabited expanses of sand
and sage and layers of ancient rock, while I remained
on canvas to be exhibited, purchased, and endlessly
reproduced. So let me set things straight: I am not
orifice, not birth-portal, and most surely not
invitation. I arise from the lineage of Michelangelo
and Fibonacci, divinely proportioned, my center
the still point from which my petals open in homage
to the nature's laws that govern a lot more than
the sex life of humans. So leave the vagina out of it.
And virginity. Whatever else I hide in there
is mine alone, and I guard it the way the skull, which
O'Keeffe also chose to paint, surrounds the secrets
of thought, feeling and sometimes genius.

Self Portrait as a Summer Cold

I am slush filling your head on a sunny day.
I am chilled fingers, labored breath, cough
so deep from the lungs it could be
prehistoric, and none of this relieved by
hot sand underfoot or a bath in the sun,
on a deck chair or towel, though the strong
drink you have an especially good excuse
to ask for—lime green, served in a frosted
goblet and graced with a paper parasol—
cuts, for a time, through the fug to ease
the cough and clear the airways. I like
strong drink. I like a salt-dusted rim
and don't mind giving way to these remedies
for the moment, but my persistence
overrides these cloudless days, this setting
where everyone else goes almost naked
in body-temperature air, relieved of
the rest of the year's stringencies, searing
processed meats over a fire and drinking
out of flasks, someone's speakers blasting
Santana, *Give me your heart, make it real or else*
forget about it, some slipping off in pairs
to do something in private, which you can't do
because you're contagious—you can't
even imagine it…. I weigh you down
like eight inches of snow in the driveway,
I am below zero outside and a fire
in the hearth, cat dead weight on the lap
while summer goes on boisterously
without you, egrets eagerly harvesting
what the tides leave, children squealing
and tireless in the waves, lovers returning

a little sheepish from the dunes. Even among
the steaming palm leaves you shiver and drift,
sip broth cooling in a paper cup, and taste
what it will be like to be old.

Self Portrait as My Nemesis

I could never be taken for a diva
or princess or damsel in distress
and in fact scorn those who wilt, prance
or preen for attention. You'd never guess
I long to be treated like a precious gem
worthy of a velvet pillow. Like the most
intriguing person in the room.

At gatherings, my first wish is to take up
no space; my next is to be surrounded by
people who want to know more and more
about me, or by partners lining up to twirl me
around the floor while everyone steps aside,
wishing they could move so lightly, spin
so brilliantly away and then melt, like warmed
silk, back into waiting arms....

In the presence of a narcissist, I shut down.
Shrink to a puddle of insignificance. I let him/
her siphon all air from the room, and marvel
at how smoothly they get away with hogging
the conversation or Zoom screen, gathering
steam, while the little *me, me, me*
simmers in secret longing.

Self Portrait as Cocktail Hour

I am ice tumbling into a bucket; spirits
harboring wise or heady secrets decanted or
shaken and served with something salty;

an hour carved out for conversation
at one remove from the day just ending,
congenial in company or ruminative over a book;

shared news or silence as dusk descends around
a wicker-furnished porch, or by a fire sending whiffs
of pine around the damask sofa and drop-leaf table.

A young father loosens his tie; a young mother sips
scotch-and-water while reading to their toddler
about elephants and gnomes, fairy dust blending

with the sound of ice in their tumblers
that resonates in the grown child's memory....
I am *hour*—not hours—not pretext for killing a bottle

or numbing the mind, and not what has morphed
into *happy hour*, all aimless flirtation and half-priced
well drinks. When observed as mindful pause, I am

the sacrament that wipes the day's slate clean.

Self Portrait as a Recipe
for Vegetarians with Food Allergies

I am the tactful map through a minefield
where gluten, tomatoes, or dairy might cause
apocalypse. Always, I seek middle ground,
my credentials based on brown rice, whole oats
and almond milk. Sometimes I get bored
and mildly bristle: what about Spanish chevre
and cage-free eggs? What, besides tomatoes,
eggplant and potatoes, is a nightshade no-no?
Can't I slip in a bit of trout or salmon when the soul,
unbeknownst to the body is feeling puckish?

I have learned to make do: fresh garlic, dill,
cilantro, cumin, herbs imported from Provence
and often, a generous pinch of Himalayan salt.
I pride myself for the trust I inspire and basically
deserve, even as I'm tempted at times to experiment
with anchovy, or broth from a duck breast

braised overnight....I take care to prevent
anaphylactic disasters caused by genuine miswiring
and indulge the lesser concerns of those in thrall
to the placebo effect, who think they can control
what befalls them by controlling what they
consume. I get it; I too, align with clearing
inner Feng Shui, wishing (in vain) the whole
overweight, embattled, toxified world might be
cleansed by larders full of low-fat, non-dairy, gluten-
free, astronomically priced organic essentials.

Self Portrait as a Recycled Wedding Outfit

Un-accessorized, I can pass unnoticed
in a crowd of sequins and off-the-shoulder
confections, my shirtwaist collar timeless, long
sleeves rolled up partway, black chiffon

backdrop modestly lit with blooms in muted
russets and golds. It's the chiffon that gives me
cachet, along with a fitted waistline whose
alteration costs more than I did on sale.

I am age-appropriate, my wearer
the contemporary of aunts, uncles
and parents' friends, and thus content—
almost—with leaving the real plumage

to the bride's attendants, all dewy decolletage,
supple limbs and upswept hair. My needs
require but a glint of rhinestone or pearl
at the throat, but I lobby for earrings

that have something to *say*—diamond clusters
or bursts of gold branches sporting buds of crystal,
all heirloom clip-ons that pinch and must be
taken off by the time the cake is cut.

When another invitation appears
my wearer need not head for the one
high-end store in town to purchase
something she will not wear twice—

you could say I one-up Houdini, deft
at slipping *into* boxes labeled Black Tie,
Black Tie Optional, and Cocktail Attire—
a tactful shape-shifter, rather than escapee.

Self Portrait with a Second Language

I live by experiment
and error—mostly
desperation—groping
blindly through the market
or bakery where everyone
counts the right change without
a second thought

and swimming—
no, treading water—
through the streets and busses
where conversation rivers
around me. I reach for phrases
and try to hold on as they slip
and slip away, leaving me

with flotsam that falls apart
as it, too, moves beyond
anything that makes sense.
I live by loneliness
and longing. I am all pause,
m-dash, and stutter, though
the mind seethes with nuance,

wit and insight—all this
lost in subject-verb pairings
trapped in the present tense
and nouns given life-support
with clumsy hand gestures—and
never mind pronouns…. Still,
in a crunch, I sometimes scare up

a functional phrase in Spanish—and once
when French blocked all my circuits

in yet another country, I was so relieved
to find a cab whose driver hailed
from Madrid, I couldn't stop holding forth—
the river that had almost drowned me
now bearing me on its raft.

Self Portrait as My Deepest Secret

Is deep as galaxies that dissolved eons ago

thus born before language, my sliver of solid ground

thus may speak in visions, like ghost-bison and sacrificial hunters
etched in the firelit privacy of caves.

Has no box, body, or country. No longing to be touched, cradled, or
spoken to. No transgression or shameful tic hidden like a filched loaf
under a cape.

Does not offer revelation—leave that to the long history of inks,
parchments, card catalogues smelling of oak and varnish….

Harbors no regrets—already I forget what I would erase or do over.

May shape itself along the contours of rivers and mountain roads, or
pulsations of polar light, all dance and disappearance—

like lithium and neon, remains of gasses, collisions and accidents that
made the universe—my secret and I are 13 billion years old—

no wonder I lean towards wave and sine, remnants my hand would
pass right through

but might I coax them, it, to rest briefly in my palm?

Self Portrait as a Recurring Dream

As if you were not the *you* of your waking hours,
that familiar knot of anxieties and what if's that flare

when you're about to leave home and only subside
once you've stuffed packing cubes with every possible

solution to family weirdness or a freak storm or a conference
where it's easy to imagine no one will talk to you,

I make you leave your maroon Osprey suitcase in the trunk
of a stranger's car; on a station platform

in the middle of nowhere (how many years now
since you boarded a train?); inside your locked door.

Every journey looms as an ending—*Goodbye, goodbye,*
I miss myself already, the maroon suitcase your only ballast

in a future without signposts, without destination, and you
no longer the person you were when you left home....

But each time you wake back in your room with its
its two dressers and stuffed closet, shaking me off

like needles of sleet, another you may be striding
out of sight with a tent, toothbrush, jar of face cream,

extra socks and a book, not minding what others think,
knowing you'll stumble on a safe place to spend the night

and savoring the ruts, hillocks, even the occasional
crumble of slope beneath your sturdy shoes....

Acknowledgments

Thanks to Ron Slate and *On the Seawall* for first publishing "Self
Portrait as an O'Keeffe Flower" and "Self Portrait as a Vermeer
Painting."

Thanks to Andrea Watson for her inspiring self-portrait workshop
in which she showed wonderful examples and then provided a list of
self-portraits to try. This book would not have been possible without
that workshop.

Photo by Jim O'Donnell

Leslie Ullman is the author of seven poetry collections, most recently *Unruly Tree* (a collection based on Brian Eno's Oblique Strategies) and a hybrid compilation of craft essays and writing exercises titled *Library of Small Happiness.* Professor Emerita at U.T.-El Paso, she serves on the faculty in the low-residency MFA program at Vermont College of the Fine Arts. Her awards include the Yale Series of Younger Poets Award, the Iowa Poetry Prize, and two NEA fellowships.